# COMMUNITY BOARD

Grego

Karen

**GARDEN CLUB**

**FREE LOANS**

**Shopping List**

**Junk or Treasure? Auction**

Aug. 23

**Spare Timers Quartet**

Yoga by The Pond

Jillian

0-123 457

**Edible Rocks**

**Cottage RENTAL**

4 Rickety Ln.

**Leech Pond Swim Lessons**

**Bird Watch Club**

**ACORN SCOUTS ADVENTURE CLUB**
*DEN MOTHER NEEDED*

**FOR SALE**

WAGON RIDES

**Lawn Care**

**RENTALS**

# Bruce's BIG STORM

RYAN T. HIGGINS

Disney • HYPERION
Los Angeles  New York

For Harrison, the littlest Higgins

A great BIG thank-you to Joanna, Griffin, Cece, Annie, and Ame for their help on this book!
And also to Dan and Mike for distracting me from working on it.

First Edition, September 2019 • 10 9 8 7 6 5 4 3 2 1 • FAC-029191-19158 • Printed in Malaysia

This book is set in Macarons/Fontspring with hand-lettering by Ryan T. Higgins
Designed by Mary Claire Cruz
Illustrations were created using scans of treated clayboard for textures,
    graphite, ink, and Photoshop

Library of Congress Cataloging-in-Publication Data

Names: Higgins, Ryan T., author, illustrator.
Title: Bruce's big storm / Ryan T. Higgins.
Description: First edition. • Los Angeles ; New York : Disney-Hyperion, 2019.
    • Summary: Grumpy Bruce the bear does not like neighbors, but is forced
    to help when a big storm draws them all to his home.
Identifiers: LCCN 2018057038• ISBN 9781368026222 (hardcover) • ISBN
    1368026222 (hardcover)
Subjects: • CYAC: Neighbors—Fiction. • Forest animals—Fiction.
    • Bears—Fiction. • Storms—Fiction. • Humorous stories.
Classification: LCC PZ7.H534962 Bry 2019 • DDC [E]—dc23
LC record available at https://lccn.loc.gov/2018057038

Reinforced binding
Visit www.DisneyBooks.com

Bruce was a bear who did not like neighbors.

Neighbors were loud.

VROOOM!

VROOOOM!

They were always interrupting ...

and pestering.

Bruce's neighbors were always coming and going, but at least none of them stayed very long . . . until the day of the big storm.

Bruce did not want visitors.

He wanted to wait out the storm in peace and quiet.

As the rain started to fall,
and the winds got windier,
more and more animals
began to arrive.

Finally, the whole neighborhood was there.

"Wait!" said Rupert. "Someone is still outside!"

There was a little bunny
out in the storm.

"Someone has to save her!" shouted Thistle.

"I'm on my way!" said Nibbs as he ran out the door.

But the big storm was
too much for the mouse,

Nibbs's rescue mission . . .

... was not going as planned.

I'm here to rescue you ... but I need help down first.

They needed a little more help.

Everyone had
to pitch in . . .

. . . and together, they pulled the bunny,
the mouse, and the grumpy old bear
back to safety—along with the umbrella.

It had been quite an adventure.

Bruce did not like adventures.

While the storm raged on outside,
Bruce's visitors, cozy and warm,
played games to pass the time.

Duck, duck,
BRUCE!
You're it!

Bruce did not like games.

CRASH

Then, one last guest arrived. . . .

A great big oak tree, and it didn't knock.

Still, everyone found a safe, dry corner to spend the night.

Come morning, Bruce's house didn't look so great.

Soon, Bruce's neighbors went back to their own homes,

leaving Bruce behind to grumble in the rubble.

But not for long . . .

All of Soggy Hollow, every neighbor, came back . . .

. . . to lend a hand, hoof, paw, or wing to help Bruce rebuild.

Over time, Bruce's house
was put back together
even better than before.